THE UNITED STATES
COAST GUARD

by Tracy Vonder Brink

PEBBLE
a capstone imprint

Pebble Explore is published by Pebble, an imprint of Capstone.
1710 Roe Crest Drive, North Mankato, Minnesota 56003
www.capstonepub.com

Library of Congress Cataloging-in-Publication Data
Names: Vonder Brink, Tracy, author.
Title: The United Sates Coast Guard / by Tracy Vonder Brink.
Description: North Mankato, Minnesota : Pebble, 2021. | Series: All about branches of the U.S. military | Includes bibliographical references and index. | Audience: Ages 6-8 | Audience: Grades 2-3 | Summary: "The U.S. Coast Guard responds to about 20,000 search-and-rescue cases a year. Its members also play an important role in enforcing the nation's laws. Learn about the roles of Coast Guard members and their training, and get an inside look at the different types of ships, aircraft, and equipment this branch uses to complete its important missions around the world"-- Provided by publisher.
Identifiers: LCCN 2020025653 (print) | LCCN 2020025654 (ebook) | ISBN 9781977131744 (library binding) | ISBN 9781977155078 (pdf)
Subjects: LCSH: United States. Coast Guard--Juvenile literature.
Classification: LCC VG53 .V66 2021 (print) | LCC VG53 (ebook) | DDC 363.28/60973--dc23
LC record available at https://lccn.loc.gov/2020025653
LC ebook record available at https://lccn.loc.gov/2020025654

Image Credits
U.S. Coast Guard Pacific Area courtesy photo, 27 (Bottom); U.S. Coast Guard photo by Aux. William Greer, Cover, NyxoLyno Cangemi, 13 (Bottom), 20, PA3 Annie R. Berlin, 7, PA3 Carleen Drummond, 17 (Bottom), Petty Office 1st Class Timothy Tamargo, 29 (Bottom), Petty Officer 1st Class Adam Eggers, 24, Petty Officer 1st Class Emaia Rise, 10, Petty Officer 1st Class Jon-Paul Rios, 23 (Top), Petty Officer 1st Class Karlton Rebenstorf, 23, (Bottom), 27 (Top), Petty Officer 2nd Class Jordan Akiyama, 16, Petty Officer 2nd Class Lisa Ferdinando, 13 (Top), Petty Officer 3rd Class Andrea L. Anderson, 15 (Bottom), Petty Officer 3rd Class Brandon Blackwell, 9, Petty Officer 3rd Class Brian McCrum, 25, Petty Officer 3rd Class Joshua Canup, 29 (Top), Petty Officer 3rd Class Steve Strohmaier, 19, Petty Officer 3rd Class Travis Magee, 15 (Top), Seaman Erik Villa Rodriguez, 5, Seaman Josalyn Brown, 8, Telfair H. Brown, Sr., 17 (Top); U.S. Coast Guard photo courtesy of Coast Guard Air Station Traverse City, 21

Design Elements
Capstone; Shutterstock: CRVL, Zerbor

Editorial Credits
Editor: Carrie Sheely; Designer: Kayla Rossow; Media Researcher: Jo Miller; Production Specialist: Laura Manthe

All internet sites appearing in back matter were available and accurate when this book was sent to press.

Printed and bound in the United States of America. PO3837

Table of Contents

Words in **bold** are in the glossary.

WHAT IS THE COAST GUARD?

The United States Coast Guard mostly works at sea and on waterways. It catches people who break laws. It makes sure people use boats safely. It also saves people who need help in the water.

The Coast Guard is one branch of the U.S. **military**. It formed more than 200 years ago. More than 40,000 people are in the Coast Guard.

JOINING THE COAST GUARD

Some Coast Guard members are on active duty. They work full-time. To join this group, people must be 17 to 31 years old. Other members are in the Coast Guard Reserve. They work part-time. They must be between 17 and 40 years old.

People who want to join the Coast Guard must be healthy, fit, and know how to swim. U.S. **citizens** can join. Some noncitizens living lawfully in the United States can also join.

New members go to basic training. It takes eight weeks. They learn to use **weapons**. They exercise hard. They learn to work together.

rescue swimmer

After basic training, each member gets a job. Some become **rescue swimmers**. Some learn to fix boats. Others make sure people on the water follow laws. The U.S. Coast Guard has more than 15 kinds of jobs.

Coast Guard members get on a plane for deployment.

Members work at bases or stations. The largest base is in Kodiak, Alaska. Some bases and stations are used for Coast Guard planes. Others are used for boats. Coast Guard members and their families live near the base or station.

Coast Guard members might need to go overseas on **missions**. Then they are **deployed**. They must leave their home base or station. They can be gone three months or longer.

COAST GUARD UNIFORMS AND GEAR

Coast Guard members have different uniforms. They wear Operational Dress Uniforms for work. They wear other uniforms for special events.

Some gear helps keep members safe. They wear life jackets. These keep members afloat if they fall in the water. Sometimes members go where it is very cold. They wear suits to stay warm and dry. The suits have layers. They can keep members warm if they fall in icy water.

Divers need special gear. They wear wet suits. The suits keep them warm in cold water. They wear scuba gear. It includes a tank with air to breathe underwater. Masks keep water out of their eyes.

Divers and rescue swimmers can wear fins. The fins help them move quickly in the water.

fins

wet suit

air tank

Some gear helps with water rescues. A rescue swimmer wears a harness when being lowered and raised from a helicopter. It has pockets to hold gear such as a flashlight, knife, and strobe light. The bright strobe light can be used to help the helicopter pilot see the swimmer.

camera system

Camera systems on vehicles can help find people in trouble. Some can show heat. People's bodies give off heat. The cameras can help find people in the water.

COAST GUARD VEHICLES

The Coast Guard has many vehicles. Members use some to catch lawbreakers. They use others for rescues.

A cutter is any Coast Guard boat that is at least 65 feet (20 meters) long. The Famous-class cutter is 270 feet (82 m) long. Its crew often lives on the boat for 6 to 8 weeks. It is used for rescues and to catch lawbreakers.

Famous-class cutter

The *Healy* is an even bigger cutter. It is 420 feet (128 m) long. It carries scientists to the North Pole. There is thick ice in this cold **polar** area. It stops most boats. But the cutter can break through the ice.

Healy

Mackinaw (front) on Lake Superior

The *Mackinaw* is another boat that breaks ice. It works on the Great Lakes in the northern United States. It keeps the lakes open for supply boats.

A response boat is shorter than a school bus. Its small size helps it pick up speed quickly. It can go more than 45 miles (72 kilometers) per hour.

A motor lifeboat is a rescue boat. Storms can make very high waves. The waves can make boats flip over. If a wave knocks the motor lifeboat over, the boat can flip over again by itself in 30 seconds.

motor lifeboat

The Coast Guard also flies helicopters. The MH-65 Dolphin can take off from a cutter's **deck**. It flies over the person in trouble. It can lower a rescue basket. A rescue swimmer helps the person into the basket. Then the MH-65 lifts it up.

MH-65 Dolphin

The MH-60 Jayhawk is much like the MH-65 Dolphin. But the Jayhawk can fly farther on a tank of fuel than the Dolphin can. It also carries more people inside.

25

LIFE IN THE COAST GUARD

People stay in the Coast Guard between four and eight years. Over time, they can rise in **rank**. Officers are in charge of other members.

A Coast Guard member's daily life depends on his or her job. Rescue teams answer calls for help. Others may clean up **oil** spills in the ocean. Some go on **patrol**. They make sure fishermen only catch the fish they're allowed to. They search boats for **illegal** goods.

Members of the Coast Guard are always ready to help. They train often to be at their best. They are willing to risk their lives for others. They go out in bad storms to rescue people. They catch lawbreakers. They bravely serve the country every day.

GLOSSARY

citizen (SI-tuh-zuhn)—a member of a country or state who has the right to live there

deck (DEK)—the floor of a boat or ship

deploy (di-PLOY)—to move troops into position for military action

illegal (ill-LEE-guhl)—against the law

military (MIL-uh-ter-ee)—the armed forces of a country

mission (MISH-uhn)—a military task

oil (OIL)—a thick, greasy liquid that burns easily and does not mix with water

patrol (puh-TROHL)—to protect and watch an area

polar (POH-lur)—having to do with the icy regions around the North or South Pole

rank (RAYNK)—an official position or job level

rescue swimmer (re-SKYU SWIM-ur)—someone who goes into water to save people who are in danger

weapon (WEP-uhn)—something used for fighting

READ MORE

Abdo, Kenny. *United States Coast Guard*. Minneapolis: Abdo Zoom, 2019.

Best, B. J. *Coast Guard Boats*. New York: Cavendish Square, 2018.

Koestler-Grack, Rachel A. *U.S. Coast Guard*. Mankato, MN: Amicus, 2019.

INTERNET SITES

Ducksters: U.S. Government for Kids: United States Armed Forces
www.ducksters.com/history/us_government/united_states_armed_forces.php

Kiddle: United States Coast Guard Facts for Kids
kids.kiddle.co/United_States_Coast_Guard

U.S. Coast Guard Facts
www.uscgboating.org/content/us-coast-guard-facts.php

INDEX